For all the people who feed Catty

A Note to Parents & Caregivers—

Reading Stars books are designed to build confidence in the earliest of readers. Relying on word repetition and visual cues, each book features fewer than 50 words.

You can help your child develop a lifetime love of reading right from the very start. Here are some ways to help your beginning reader get going:

 Read the book aloud as a first introduction

Run your fingers below the words as you read each line

Give your child the chance to finish the sentences or read repeating words while you read the rest.

Encourage your child to read aloud every day!

Every Child can be a Reading Star!

Published in the United States by Xist Publishing
www.xistpublishing.com

First Edition
eISBN: 978-1-5324-3201-9
Paperback ISBN: 978-1-5324-3202-6
Hardcover ISBN: 978-1-5324-3203-3
Printed in the United States of America

Is Catty Fast?

Juliana O'Neill

Alina Kralia

x*ist Publishing

Catty is a cat.

Catty is a fat cat.

Catty is a cat that likes food.

It is not time for food.

It is time to play.

15

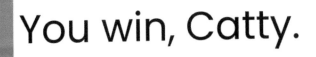

You win, Catty.

It is time for a nap.

Catty!
It is time for food.

Catty is fast.

23

Catty is a fast, fat cat.

I am a Reading Star
because I can read the
words in this book:

a	likes
cat	nap
Catty	not
fast	play
fat	that
food	time
for	to
is	win
it	you

xist Publishing